LINDA J. WAGNER
ILLUSTRATED BY SCHENKER DE LEON

Faeries at Midnight

And Other Magical Tales

Balboa Press books may be ordered through booksellers or by contacting:

Balboa Press
A Division of Hay House
1663 Liberty Drive
Bloomington, IN 47403
www.balboapress.com
844-682-1282

ISBN: 978-1-9822-6964-7 (sc)
ISBN: 978-1-9822-7057-5 (hc)
ISBN: 978-1-9822-6965-4 (e)

Library of Congress Control Number: 2021911058

Print information available on the last page.

Balboa Press rev. date: 06/17/2021

BALBOA.PRESS
A DIVISION OF HAY HOUSE

For children of all ages...

*For all my friends who listen to my tales
of magic, the fae, and the moon…*

For my son Collin Wagner, the writer, whose poems are included

Ms. Wagner is also the author of
**The Maiden's Journey
And Other Tales of Magical Creatures**

"The verses' lush imagery and the tales' yearning for connection, healing, and the divine, emphasized by flowery language, will appeal to romantics."

— review from Kirkus Indie

*"May you always feel the
magic of a faerie moon"*

Linda J. Wagner

Awakened by a flutter
A whisper with a sigh
I feel a wispy breeze
A sparkle flickers by

A giggle and a chiming
Announcing magical games
I toss aside my blanket
And interrupt my dreams

Following the light with
Quick and breathless steps
Suddenly I find myself
Within a shimmering web

Beautiful and glittery
Shimmering skies beyond
I elevate mysteriously
Floating above the ground

Weaving enchantment and music
Mixed with friendship and love
A crescendo of musical merriment
The magical night has begun

I find myself humming and singing
Dancing impetuously free
A hand reaches out to invite me
And magnetically captivates me

My gliding feet
Still above the ground
I receive invitation
To dance in the round

A faerie prince poses
Majestic and grand
I take my position
At his command

With aid from the faerie dust
Shimmering in light
Glittering sparkles
Captivate my sight

I commence with light steps
Enchanted by fae
I've been given the glamour
They invite me to stay

I enter dimensions
Unknown and surreal
Layers upon layers
Unveil to reveal

A faerie tale world
Of love and respect
For an ancient realm
Disappeared from neglect

The prince so attentive
Dips low for my hand
This world of such wonder
I now understand

He sings of romance
And tender musings
The sound of his music
So sweet and so soothing

The room starts to twirl
As he lifts me 'bove ground
Multitudes of faeries
Join in on the round

Joyously singing and
Dancing with grace
I breathlessly flow
to match their swift pace

The night travels on
As though time ne'er exists
My soul and my heart
Unable to resist

I feel myself slipping
As if there's no cure
From this magnetic realm
Of irresistible allure

The prince locks my gaze
And sincerely recites,
"You've had quite a dance
This mystical night

'Tis time to return to
Your own realm and time
You have learnt quite a truth
From this mystical rhyme."

The faeries all gathered
With glittering glances
"Goodbye, goodbye",
they ingeniously chanted.

Other beings of magic
Suddenly arrived
Unicorns, mermaids,
Sylphes, and sprites

Elves and pixies,
Guardians, knights,
Offering great cheer this
Most wondrous of nights

"We bid you return
When the moon is round
When light, magic,
And fullness abounds."

The Prince led me on
To a place in the mist
He departed with an ancient
Blessing and kiss

I could not decipher
The language of old
I could not break free
Of his powerful hold

I closed my eyes
And thought on his words
Remembering my life
In a different world

A faerie princess
Followed by her court
Grandly ascends
To sit on her throne

She raises her sceptre
I kneel at her seat
She nods her approval
And bids me retreat

I must return home
To another reality
Then I instantly felt
The pull of earth's gravity

The glamour disappeared
Without a trace
Transported home
I felt warm and safe

The glamour and glitter
Disappeared from my eyes
I had learnt a great lesson
So true and so wise

Love and enchantment
Magic and delight
Can exist in a world
Where dreams can survive

I await the bright moon
and the chime of the fae
And follow my heart
to a faraway place

A realm where love
And enchantment began
In a mystical world
In a faraway land

A faerie tale world
So alluring and free
A fantastical place
For you and for me

The End

Other magical tales…

By, Linda J. Wagner
and
Collin Wagner

Don't Forget to Dream

Don't forget to dream, my love
Don't forget to dream

Tho' the waves are wildly churning
The sea defies the storm
Your dreams will always conquer
The storm inside your soul

What is that you fear the most?
What is that, my child?

The crashing waves will soon subside
And you will find once more
A treasure chest left by the tide
Has washed up on the shore

Gems of gold and jewels of light
Seashells from a secret world
Look in your heart and there your dreams
Like miracles will unfold

Magical House by the Sea

For Aileen

Skies of blue with cotton candy white
The sea with silvery, sparkly light
Sandy shores of shimmering gleam
A glowing image of a child's dream

The mermaids and dolphins whisper, "Come near!"
The sea captain's laughter so cheerful and clear
"Can we live by the sea, forever and a day?"
Then God said, "My dear, we shall find you a way!"

Beckoning entry into this wondrous home
A beautiful angel appears at the door
Never to doubt beauty and peace
We shall dwell here forever
Near the magical sea

The Shadows

The shadows conceal in the dark of night
Within they hold a powerful light
The mysteries of old concealed well
The test of time will always tell

A familiar word you now seek
For the humble, kind, compassionate, meek
Yet the strong know just as right
What lies within The shadows of night

Darkness will never quench the light
And light will reveal the breath of life

Collin Wagner

Rite of the Night

The moon shines, its glow is bright
It is the night for the rite, tonight
Be in the air, cool and crisp
Feel the power of the will-o'-the-wisp
The mysteries float, the mysteries show
That one can see, and one can know
Perform the rite in perfect trust
In great love, under will, thou must

Draw the space, the circle if you will
Sprinkle the dust around the sill
Say the name of the Earth
Remembering who gave you birth
Hear thee, and hear thee well
For the Earth hears all, and time will tell
Draw the forms and names of old
If you wish and feel so bold

Draw the liquid, pour into the glass
The chalice of rites, let it not pass
Feel the breath of life from the night
Feel the sensation that is in the rite
Charge the soul, the body, and mind
Remember love, to be compassionate and kind
Close with a wish, a smile, and a prayer
You've performed the rite with special care

Close the space, and walk away
Return again another day
In perfect love, trust, and light
Always remember the rite of the night

Collin Wagner

Creative Projects for Faeries at Midnight

Language Arts
-Create a scrapbook of your favorite parts of the story,
or the entire plot of the story and poems
-Research and write a report or a speech about the history of
faeries in folklore and cultures around the world
-Write your own poem or story about faeries
-Read and compare other faerie tales to **Faeries at Midnight**

Art
-Draw, paint, sketch, or color your own illustrations to
your favorite parts of the story or poems
-Make doll recreations of the characters in the story using scrap materials or art materials
-Create a costume for yourself and a friend of one or more of the characters
-Create a shadow box or diorama of events of the story or poem

Science and Mathematics
-Research or study the phases of the moon
-Create a fictional explanation of the faerie traveling to a
different time and place

Music
-Write a song and create music for the story or poems

Physical Education
-Create your own faerie dance
-What are some of your ideas you can create from the stories?
-Spend a day living as a faerie or magical creature

Classroom discussions and activities for Faeries at Midnight

-List examples of the following poetic and literary devices from the story and poems:

Rhyme
Imagery
Mood
Onomatopoeia
Personification
Hyperbole
Alliteration
Theme
Genre

-What is the mood of the story? Is it happy, hopeful, exciting? What examples can you give from the story?

-Is the plot suspenseful, adventurous, mysterious? What examples can you give from the story?

-What is the theme of the story? There can be more than one! Explain your answer and give examples

Give each character a name and describe or sketch each one!

The girl-

The kitty cat-

The prince-

The faerie dancers-

The magical creatures-

The faerie queen-

The lady and the man by the house-

The girl and the unicorn-

Note and sketch page for your own ideas

Note and sketch page for your own ideas

Write your own magical story or poem!

The Magical End!

Printed in the United States
by Baker & Taylor Publisher Services